Parables from the Holy Spirit

Jessica Sims

DEDICATION

To all the friends and family who continue to
encourage me in writing.
Most of all to my Lord and Savior Jesus Christ.

Table of Contents

The Eternal Conversation

Let me tell you a little secret.

Come on. Lean in a little.

You have been lied to for the majority of your life.

Okay. I get it. You're already a few sentences into this passage, and I throw this at you. You were expecting to read stories of who knows what. Hold your horses now. I promise you it's coming. Don't go closing the book before you even started, and don't skip over this. I just want to talk to you first.

So when I say that you have been lied to for the majority of your life, I don't mean it in the way that you think...maybe. I'm talking about your faith in God and what He has done for you. The world loves to paint a certain picture of Christianity. A picture of religiosity. A picture of tradition. A picture of...rules. Well, I'm here to tell you that believing in Jesus and accepting Him as your personal Savior is not like that. It is a relationship. He comes to you as a friend with a desire to know you personally and for you to know Him personally. He wants to show you that knowing Him is just like knowing a best friend or a family member but closer. He knows everything about you because He created you, and He loves you dearly. He loved you enough to go to the cross for you.

"'For God so loved the world that He gave His only begotten Son, that whoever believes in Him should not perish but have everlasting life. For God did not send His

Son into the world to condemn the world, but that the world through Him might be saved.'"
-    John 3:16-17 NKJV

These words were straight from Jesus's mouth. The mouth of the One who died for you, so that you could be reconciled to the Heavenly Father. In beginning your faith journey, put aside all of the preconceived notions about rules and traditions. Just give Him a chance to properly and officially introduce Himself.

Let me tell you another lie that people believe. People in general believe that God doesn't speak. There are so many wrongs in the world. So many hardships. So many tragedies that occur daily that it is supposedly obvious to conclude that God is silent and complacent about everything and has left us to our own devices. Any of that sound familiar? All of that is indeed a lie. God cares about the condition of our lives, and He is always speaking. In fact, He is even speaking to you now through many people that you know and love. The question is...are you truly listening?

"For since the creation of the world His invisible attributes are clearly seen, being understood by the things that are made, even His eternal power and Godhead, so they are without excuse,..."
-    Romans 1:20 NKJV

"For God may speak in one way, or in another, yet man does not perceive it."

- Job 33:14 NKJV

Think about it this way...when you are an artist or a creator of some sort, wouldn't you have a signature of some sort to show that what you created was indeed originally crafted by your own hands. That instinct to mark what we have created does not originally come from us, but from our Heavenly Father. Plus, we cherish the art that we create, and the Father in Heaven is no different. We were made in His image, so naturally we would have habits and attributes like His without even realizing it. The entirety of the world is covered in His signature, even the condition of our bodies to handle many things. Sickness. Poison. All of it. God created us perfectly so that we would be taken care of in every way possible. So with the care and time that He took to create us and the world that we inhabit, do you really think that He is a someone who is careless?

Just like in the scripture above, the whole of nature sings of His glory and majesty. People who spend a lot of time enjoying nature tend to come to the conclusion of a wonderful God having been the creator of it all. His signature is everywhere. His marksmanship is everywhere we look. We can hear His voice anywhere and everywhere. The question is...are you really listening? The conversation that our Father in Heaven started in Genesis with "Let there be light" is still continuing today. Tune your ears to God's voice and join in the eternal conversation with our Heavenly Father and Creator.

"'He who has ears to hear, let him hear!'"
-    Matthew 11:15 NKJV

Absolutely Filthy

We come to a small town, and in that small town is a local restaurant that is constantly packed every day of the week. This restaurant has food that is so good that it reminds anyone who walks in the doors of the taste of home. The restaurant is not only a place of business, but a refuge for the town's youth. They love to gather in the restaurant over snacks and coffee and listen to the owner's stories and various pieces of wisdom.

One day, the restaurant had a particularly slow day where almost no one came in. When no one comes to dine, it is the perfect opportunity for the town youth to get uninterrupted stories from the owner. So the owner had time to talk. Before they ate, he asked them to say a blessing over the food with him. They followed suit.

All: ...Amen.

After saying grace, the youth looked at the owner and asked him, "Why do you always say grace before every meal?" So the owner began to explain.

Owner: I say grace because I want to acknowledge and show gratefulness to the One that gave me this food.

The Youth: Who is that? The business men?

Owner: No! It's not the businessmen. It is our Heavenly Father on high who knows all and sees all.

The Youth: What's there to be grateful for? It's just food.

Owner: Well, there is so much more that we have to be thankful for because of God Almighty on high.

The Youth: What else?

Owner: Well, He sent His only Son Jesus Christ to die for us so that we could be cleansed from our sins.

The Youth: Sin? What's sin?

At that question, the owner was very much delighted and ready to answer. So he grabbed a nearby chair, pulled it up to the table, and sat down as he began his elaborate explanation...

For starters, I have to first explain the level of holiness that the Heavenly Father holds. Imagine holiness as a level of cleanliness, and the Father in Heaven has a whole lot of it. His house and His courts are absolutely spotless. You would never find one spec of dust or a spot of dirt wherever He resides. Not only is His house spick and span spotless, but He is the very definition of cleanliness. His cleanliness is on a level where anything that has a single spot or spec of dirt no matter how small will be destroyed in the blink of an eye. It is destroyed because His level of cleanliness is so perfect that it just swallows up dirt. No spec of dirt can even be in the same place that He resides because He is, in fact, the definition of cleanliness, and He would never allow any spec of dirt to taint the place He indwells. That is holiness.

Now sin is the exact opposite of the Heavenly Father's cleanliness in every way possible. The one thing I fail to mention is that this cleanliness and filthiness is not physical. It is in a place that is not visible to our eyes. Even though we can't see it, it leaves traces in ways that we can see. But the Father can see it all, tangible and intangible. So with holiness equating to cleanliness, sin equates to filthiness. Sin is the level of filthiness that isn't like being covered in dirt after a nice day playing in the mud and grass. No. No. No. Sin is dirt that stinks to high Heaven, and because the Father can see all, you not only stink to Him, but you look filthy too.

To start off...sin smells like a dog's hind quarters after giving a nice gift in a plastic bag to its owner during a long walk. Then you combine that smell with the hind quarters of another dog that just did the same thing.

It doesn't just stop there. Combine that smell I just described with that same dog's breath after it has lapped up the water out of a used toilet then proceeds to go and eat its own vomit and poop. It is near impossible to get a dog's breath smelling normal after that. That's what sin smells like.

Sin smells like the moldy, expired cheese that you left in the back of the fridge. Oh, but it doesn't stop there. Sin is like that same moldy, expired cheese left out on the counter for weeks on end, then you take that festering cheese, and put it on the sidewalk on the hottest day in August. Can't you just imagine the stench that it would have by then? Not only is the stench absolutely awful, but the look of it would be horrific. Considering that it was already moldy, that mold would have grown more and more hairy, and it wouldn't even look like cheese anymore. Just a green hairy mess that you wouldn't know what to do with. Also since you left the cheese on the sidewalk in the hot sun, you can imagine that all types of critters such as beetles, cockroaches, and maggots have made their home in the "used to be cheese" monstrosity. Would you touch that after so long? I can imagine that you would just leave it right there on the sidewalk for the lowest bottom-feeders.

At these words, the youth paused in eating, but continued to listen to the owner...

As I stated before, sin is not just dirt, it's absolute filth. Imagine sin to be the dirtiest alley in the filthiest city that you could ever imagine. That alley doesn't just have trash. That alley has trash and a whole bunch of critters that you never thought would live there. Rats in the tens, fifties, and hundreds in just one corner in the back of the alley. Along with the critters living in every other corner of that alley, you have garbage cans of food that has been sitting in the trash can for weeks on end with no hope of sanitation picking it up. Not only is the trash weeks old, but more and more trash is piled onto that old trash until the garbage can is overflowing to a point where the trash is falling on the ground and just stays there. In that same alley, the stray dogs, stray cats, and whatever other stray animals exist have made their home in every nook and cranny of that alley, not counting the rat corner. Not only have they made those nooks and crannies their places to sleep, but places to relieve themselves. Fresh droppings everywhere. Because they are strays, their marked territory remains for no one to clean it. Those stray animals shed everywhere, and there is no one to sweep it up.

Now with that being sin, imagine yourself having been in the alley with everything I described plus that old sidewalk moldy cheese all over the ground of that alley, and not only do you stand in that alley, but you roll on the ground of that alley amongst that moldy cheese, those critters, that hair, and that filth. When you get off the ground after rolling around, how do you think you will be? I'll tell you how you will be! Absolutely filthy is what you will be! That is exactly what the sin nature of mankind is. You stink to high Heaven, and you are absolutely filthy! How do you think the Father in Heaven, who is the ultimate cleanliness will react when He sees you? Not only do you have filth that He can see, but you stink all the way from earth to high Heaven. That stench and filth is not just any stench. It is a stench that would even make the most experienced health inspector tremble.

Would you put up with that stench? If there was any object that had that much filth and stench in your rooms, would you try to save it by throwing some hot soap and water on it, or would you just throw it away saying that it's a waste to even try? I can bet my bottom dollar that you would throw it away without a second thought.

But that is the goodness of the Heavenly Father and the goodness of His Son. Even though the Heavenly Father sees your absolute filth and smells you all the way to the ninth Heaven, He doesn't see you as a waste. He would never throw you away. Because He is the ultimate definition of cleanliness, He knows exactly how to get rid of every spec of dirt and waft of stench on you. You can't clean yourself because you would only muddy the process with the filth that covers you. So, His Son Jesus Christ was sent to clean you. He washes you white as snow with His blood that takes away that stench and filth of sin and completely cleans you to where you have the same cleanliness that He does. Not only does Jesus clean you, but He gives you instructions on how to stay clean. Even if you get dust on you while trying to follow His instructions, His Grace through the blood with which He has already cleansed you can clean you again. But the only difference is that the Holy Spirit will stop you from ever returning to that filthy alley again.

At the end of this description, the youth looked at the owner in amazement, disgust, and wonder unable to take another bite because of the horrific description they had just heard. The owner looked at their faces and said, "I take it that you want your food to-go?" So the owner packed up all of their food, handed it to them, and the youth paid their tabs. Everyone exchanged thank yous and goodbyes, and the youth left the restaurant feeling as if they needed a good, long scrub in the shower.

The Woman Who was Loved

We come to a large city where a young woman lives.
This woman had a wonderful life, a beautiful home to live
in, a wonderful family that loved her, and a successful
career in the field of her dreams. She had it all.

What those closest to her didn't know was…
She was broken on the inside. Beaten down by the
lingering trauma from the hardships she had overcome.
"I will never forgive them for all the pain they caused
me!"

Insecure about her work…
"I have to be the best. Everything must be perfect. I can't
slip up again."

Questioning her loved ones…
"What are their intentions? What do they mean? I don't
trust them."

And struggling to love herself…
"I ain't worth a dime."

Every night these thoughts plagued her mind.
So much so that she often slipped into a depressive stupor
and drank at night crying herself to sleep from the
overwhelming self-loathing.

No one knew about the self-hate that she constantly
carried because she hid it so well behind a positive veil.

"You can do it!"
"Just believe in yourself!"
"You're almost there!"

Until one day, she was walking by herself with these thoughts constantly swirling in her head. At the same time, a man on the street walks up to her...
"Excuse me, ma'am. I just wanted to tell you that you that Jesus Christ loves you dearly."

The young woman says, "Oh umm. Thank you."
Without realizing the seed that had just been planted, she continues walking to work.

As she was walking alone, she suddenly hears...

"He's right, you know..."

"Huh?" Said the woman.

She looks up in surprise as a Man stands next to her.

"He's right, you know. That I love you very much."

The woman stares at the Man in bewilderment.
His eyes were filled with Light, and He seemed to have a Light surrounding Him.

"Excuse me?"

The Man says,

"For God so loved the world that He gave His only begotten Son, that whoever believes in Him should not perish but have everlasting life."
-    John 3:16 NKJV

"Who are you?"

"Who do you think I Am?" The Man says.

"I don't know who you are. Now leave me alone."

She continues to walk, but the Man calmly walks next to her.

"What are you doing?"

"I would like to walk you to work."

Sensing no harm from this Man, the woman begrudgingly lets Him walk her. As the woman walks into her building, a young man walks up to her. Now you can imagine this man as the office flirt. Always trying to catch the next woman. The young man hands her a flower.

"Greetings, my darling."

"Hello." The woman says with a slight blush.

As this is transpiring, the Man next to her starts to chime in...

"I can offer you so much more than that. He doesn't care about you in the slightest. You are a treasure to me, my love."

At those words, the woman turns around to ask Him, "What are you doing?"

Then the young man chimes in, "What is who doing?"

"Can't you see Him? The Man standing right here with the Light in His eyes?" Said the woman.

The young man just stares at the woman in confusion and walks away without another word.

With that, the Man chimes in, "No one can see or hear me but you, my love."

At that comment, the woman goes to work. At the end of the day, the woman comes home with the Man still next to her.

"Who are You? Why are You here?"

To answer her questions, the Man says, "I am the One who truly loves you."

Still not sure what that meant, the young woman gets ready for bed.

That night, the young woman had the same self-loathing thoughts swirling around her head. The Man could tell what she was thinking and told her,
"I love you. You are treasured by Me and precious to Me. Remember that I loved you so much that I chose to die for you because you are worth it to Me." Hearing this, the young woman's thoughts calm down, and she drifts to sleep.

Another day passes as the woman goes to work and comes home with the Man staying by her side. As she heads home, the young woman asks the Man, "Seriously? Why do you stay by my side 24/7? I don't even need you here with me. I'm fine."

"Well, I stay with you because I have promised to never leave you nor forsake you," says the Man.

"...For He Himself has said, 'I will never leave you nor forsake you.'"
    -    Hebrews 13:5 NKJV

He continues…"Are you sure you're fine? I hear your thoughts. Why don't you see how much you are loved?"

So the woman tells Him everything about herself and why she feels the way she feels with Him listening to every word. As she tells Him all that was going on in her head, she began to open her heart.
The day comes to a close, and the young woman goes to sleep. The night passes, and the day passes as the woman

comes home. This time she feels heavy from the day's troubles. She comes home and begins to drink her sorrows away…

The Man appears and says, "My love, what are you doing?"

"I can't do this anymore. You keep saying that you love me, but how can you love a mess like me? I don't even have the confidence to succeed in my job. You're clearly someone special, so you should stop hanging around me. I don't want to taint that Light around You."

"Greater love has no one than this, than to lay down one's life for his friends." Says the Man.
    -    John 15:13

"Stop it," says the woman.

"…'Behold! The Lamb of God who takes away the sin of the world!'"
    -    John 1:29 NKJV

"STOP IT!" Says the young woman.

"I've already done this for you because I love you," says the Man.

"I'm not good enough! I'm afraid I'm gonna mess everything up like I always do. I ain't worth a dime!" Says the woman.

"You aren't worth a dime because you are worth more than a diamond. You are priceless. You are My treasure, and you are Mine."

The woman sinks to the floor with tears streaming down her face.

"I can fix the broken and make you new," says the Man wiping away her tears.

After hearing this...
The woman finally begins to see...

"Jesus," she says.

He smiles. Happy that she realized Who He was.

"I love You, Jesus."

The young woman gets up with a new found strength. "Okay, Jesus. What's next?"

...

"Jesus?"

The woman looks around, but couldn't see Him anywhere. Then she walks into the kitchen and looks at the table. On the table was a huge beautiful bouquet of blossoming red roses in a vase with a Bible next to them and a note saying...

I will always be with you.
Love,
Jesus Christ

19

The Other Me

I am just your average, every day person with your average, every day life. I have a job. I have a place to rest my head, and I have family and friends who love me. If you looked at my life, you would see it as a lifestyle that almost anyone has because it is about as ordinary as you can get. There is one problem, however…there is another me.

When I say another me, I don't mean that I have a twin. No. I was born an only child. No, I don't have a long-lost twin. Believe me when I say that I already checked that. By another me, I mean it *is* me, but it *isn't* me. I look at *her* and see my eyes, my hair, my nose…everything on my face…but *she's not* me.

The other me is completely opposite of me. *She* never smiles. *She* communicates audibly through gruesome sneers and growls yet *she* somehow always knows and understands what I'm thinking. There is no reasoning with *her* at all. *She* is everything that I despise about myself. All my insecurities, my jealousies, my hatred, my unforgiveness, my malice…
I cringe just thinking about it. But this is *her*. The carnal me.

I have always had a relationship with the carnal me for as long as I can remember. Even though I have known *her* for so long, we have never developed a loving relationship. We always fought with each other every minute of every day. It gets so confusing and frustrating that I can't decide what to do half the time.

"For the flesh lusts against the Spirit, and the Spirit against the flesh; and these are contrary to one another, so that you do not do the things that you wish."
  -    Galatians 5:17 NKJV

In this complicated relationship that I have with *her*, I have come to know that *she* doesn't care about me one way or another. In fact, *she* always goes out of *her* way to try and ruin my life. By anger...

Mom: Honey, are you okay? I know that you're upset that I said no, but please understand that it's for your own goo—

Her: No! I can't believe you! How could you do this to me?! You don't love me! I hate you!

By sadness...

Friend: Hey, I know these past few days have been hard on you, but just hang in there. Things will get better.

Her: No they won't. Things will never get better. It will always be the same thing over and over. I'm tired of it. Just leave me alone.

By despair...

Her: No one loves you. No one cares about you. Maybe it's best that you're not around.

She says and does everything that *she* possibly can to ruin my life. *She* tries to destroy me at every turn. I hate *her*. I hate *her* with a dying passion. I don't want to hurt my family. I don't want to ruin my relationships with the friends that I hold dear, but I can't seem to stop...*her*.

"For what I am doing, I do not understand. For what I will to do, that I do not practice; but what I hate, that I do."
- 	Romans 7:15 NKJV

I plan to make an escape. I want to get away from *her*. But how...?

Preacher: "Therefore if the Son makes you free, you shall be free indeed."
- 	John 8:36 NKJV

Freedom? Does that mean my life isn't ruined by *her*? I had to know more, so I started reading the book the preacher was reading.

As I read the book, I learned so much about redemption...

"In Him we have redemption through His blood, the forgiveness of sins, according to the riches of His grace..."
- 	Ephesians 1:7 NKJV

I learned a lot about Grace...

"For by grace you have been saved through faith, and that not of yourselves; it is the gift of God, not of works, lest anyone should boast."
-    Ephesians 2:8-9 NKJV

And most importantly salvation...

"...that if you confess with your mouth the Lord Jesus and believe in your heart that God has raised Him from the dead, you will be saved."
-    Romans 10:9 NKJV

I was thinking about all that I had read, and was starting to feel like I could finally be free from *her* until I looked in the mirror...
I saw *her* in a way that I had never seen *her* before. *She* wasn't *her* usual angry self. *She* was enraged. Enraged to a point where *she* spoke...

Her: Hah. You think that Jesus fellow will help you? He won't even bat an eye for you.

Me: Maybe He'll listen to me because it says I won't be put to shame if I call on Him.

Her: Have you looked at yourself in the mirror? *I* am you. We are one. You will ruin your relationship with Him like you've ruined everything else.

At one point in this conversation...I realized something, and I think *she* knew it too and was afraid of what I would say and do.

Me: Everything that ruined my life was not because of me but because of *you*. I am not *you*.

"If, then, I do what I will not to do, I agree with the law that it is good. But now, it is no longer I who do it, but sin that dwells in me."
-       Romans 7:16-17 NKJV

Me: I am one with Christ and Christ only. *You* are nothing but sinful flesh. I will never be one with *you* again.

"But he who is joined to the Lord is one spirit with Him."
-       1 Corinthians 6:17 NKJV

Me: Jesus would never turn me away because I have faith in Him.

"For 'whoever calls on the name of the Lord shall be saved.'"
-       Romans 10:13 NKJV

Her: You can't walk away from *me*! You need *me*!

Me: I am tired of this life that I have lived with *you*! I'm done with it, and I'm done with *you*!

"For whoever desires to save his life will lose it, but whoever loses his life for My sake and the gospel's will save it."
- Mark 8:35 NKJV

Me: I don't need *you* and I will never need *you* again!

"Therefore, if anyone is in Christ, he is a new creation; old things have passed away; behold, all things have become new."
- 2 Corinthians 5:17 NKJV

Her: You think you can get rid of *me* that easily?! You can try to suppress *me*, but *I* will never go away! *I* will always be with you.

"I have been crucified with Christ; it is no longer I who live, but Christ lives in me; and the life which I now live in the flesh I live by faith in the Son of God, who loved me and gave Himself for me."
- Galatians 2:20 NKJV

Me: I am a new creation now for I have been crucified with Christ. "Get behind Me, Satan! You are an offense to Me, for you are not mindful of the things of God, but the things of men."
- Matthew 16:23 NKJV

After those words, there was a sudden bright light, and then I passed out.

Her: ...

Me: ...

I woke up and found myself lying on the floor in front of the bathroom mirror surrounded by shattered glass. I got up and looked at the mirror, and to my surprise, the gaps where the missing pieces used to be were nowhere to be found. The mirror looked as good as new...in fact, it looked better than new. I looked on the floor and saw no more glass shards, but in their place were small puddles of water that smelled like honey. I looked at the mirror with a small fear of seeing *her* staring back at me, but...I didn't see *her*. In place of *her*...I saw...**me**. I was smiling. No trace of a sneer or a growl. Just a small smile that was brighter than I had ever seen. I had such joy and peace when I finally met the other **me**...the new **me**...the new **me** in Christ.

"...that he might sanctify and cleanse her with the washing of water by the word..."
-    Ephesians 5:26 NKJV

"And do not be conformed to this world, but be transformed by the renewing of your mind, that you may prove what is that good and acceptable and perfect will of God."
-    Romans 12:2 NKJV

The Cottage

There was once a small cottage that was a refuge for all who came by. People from all walks of life passed through that cottage at least once in their lifetime. This cottage gave people the freedom to come and go as they pleased. If they stayed, then everything was shared with them. If they left, they couldn't take anything with them. This cottage was special because it was the Lord's cottage.

"A father of the fatherless, a defender of widows, is God in His holy habitation."
- Psalm 68:5 NKJV

In this cottage, lived an adorable little girl. This girl was not like any other girl. She was special because she was born in the Lord's cottage. She had no parents or family. The cottage was all that she had. She had always walked with the Lord since the day she was born and never wanted for anything. The Lord loved her very dearly. He knew her and she knew Him.

"The Lord is my shepherd; I shall not want."
- Psalm 23:1 NKJV

Little Girl: I love the cottage. This is my favorite place in the whole wide world.

Jesus: This is the only place you've ever known in the whole wide world.

Little Girl: I know. But I never want to leave this place. I wanna just stay here with You all day.

Jesus: Isn't it a bit boring just playing with me?

Little Girl: It would be nice to have others, but I don't mind. This is my most favoritest place ever.

Jesus: One of these days, I want to give you more brothers and sisters.

Little Girl: I'm gonna have siblings?!

Jesus: Of course, my little daughter. But in order to do that, there will come a day that you'll have to leave this place when you're old enough.

Little Girl: Leave? But I don't want to leave.

The little girl looked at the Lord with teary eyes and an anxious heart.

Jesus: Don't be afraid. When that day comes. You will be ready. Just know that even though you will leave this cottage for a brief moment, you can always come back to recharge because this place is your refuge.

As the days passed, the little girl grew with the Lord. In preparation for her to leave the cottage one day, He taught her all that time about Him and His relationship with her.

Jesus: I want you to remember that when you leave this cottage, it will be harder to sense my presence because of the world around you. You may not be able to sense it for a brief moment, but just know that I will always be with you holding your hand.

"Be strong and of good courage, do not fear nor be afraid of them; for the Lord your God, He is the One who goes with you. He will not leave you nor forsake you."
-    Deuteronomy 31:6 NKJV

Jesus: You might be looked at strangely because your family is not like theirs. But remember that the family you have will never disappear, and it is much more beautiful than you can ever imagine.

"And you will be hated by all for My name's sake. But he who endures to the end will be saved."
-    Matthew 10:22 NKJV

Jesus: Remember this: They may give you strange looks, but there is nothing for you to be ashamed of.

"For I am not ashamed of the gospel of Christ, for it is the power of God to salvation for everyone who believes, for the Jew first and also for the Greek. For in it the righteousness of God is revealed from faith to faith; as it is written, 'The just shall live by faith.'"
-    Romans 1:16-17 NKJV

The days grew older and older as the little girl learned with Jesus. Jesus taught her many lessons every day, and she did her best to retain them all until that one fateful day when it was time for her to step out of the cottage. Standing with her at the door, the Lord gave her all that she needed in her travels and gave her a tiny book with instructions and directions so that she could find her way back to her refuge. The time had come for her to leave, so He walked with her to the door, held her hand, and walked with her out the door. As she stepped through the threshold of the door, she had the hand of the Lord in hers, and then it disappeared. "Where did the Lord go?" She thought. Then she could hear a quiet voice within her saying, "Don't worry, my daughter. I'm right here with you and will always be." Following those words, she felt someone gently squeeze her hand.

"But the anointing which you have received from Him abides in you, and you do not need that anyone teach you; but as the same anointing teaches you concerning all things, and is true, and is not a lie, and just as it has taught you, you will abide in Him."
-    1 John 2:27 NKJV

The little girl looked around at the forest that surrounded the cottage and began to walk along the path. She walked for a while until she came to a group of small kids her age. Her face shined as she realized they were playing a game. She wanted to join them. So she walked up and waited for them to notice her.

Through all the laughter, they hadn't noticed her for a while until someone laid eyes on her, and they stopped. They looked at her and then continued playing, not paying any attention to her. A little sad, she stood there not sure what to do, hoping that they would let her play. At some point, they felt awkward and walked away from her without another word.

Watching all this transpire, another little girl the same age came up to her.

Friend: They don't like new people. Especially ones that don't look like them.

Little girl: What do you mean? Don't I look human like them.

Friend: You do, but there is a small Light in you. They don't understand what it is. What is that?

Little girl: It is my Lord. He promised me that He would stay with me all the days of my life.

At these words, the little girl described the life that she lived with Jesus to her new friend. She told her about the Lord and how He sent her into the world to bring more brothers and sisters. She told her that the Lord will welcome anyone who comes in His home. The little girl's new friend could see the joy on her face and saw that the Light in her began to shine brighter and brighter as they continued to talk. Noticing this, her new friend became curious and agreed to go back to the cottage with her.

Using the tiny book that they carried, the two girls came back to the cottage where the Lord greeted them both with open arms. The new friend was at first timid, but adjusted to the cottage life very well, and soon began to be taught by the Lord just the same as the little girl.

The two girls grew older in the Lord as the Lord continued to teach them both.

Jesus: Here. Take this bread and wine.

Handing both of the girls a small cup of grape juice and a small piece of bread. The Lord presumed to teach them about hunger.

Little girl: What is it?

Jesus: "This is My body which is given for you; do this in remembrance of Me…This cup is the new covenant in My blood, which is shed for you."
    -   Luke 22:19-20 NKJV

Jesus: When you go back out to the world. You will feel hunger, but remember that this bread will always fill you. If you ever want to satisfy your hunger, eat this bread, for the bread that is out in the world will never fully satisfy you.

The girls took the bread and wine. They drank and ate and soon felt stuffed after their small meal. They continued to grow with the Lord filling their stomachs with the bread and wine Jesus had given them. When they got a little older, it came time for them to go out again. So the Lord walked with them to the door, gave them a bag full of bread and wine, and walked with them through the door. They were off again.

They traveled through the forest together talking about the excitement they had for new brothers and sisters soon to come, then they came upon this poor married couple, a man and a woman. This couple was considered the scourge of the world. Everyone regarded them as the bottom-feeders of the world because they had absolutely nothing. No food, barely any clothes, and no place to rest their heads. The girls walked up to them, and the couple noticed the Light that was in them. Seeing how the Light was so bright, they were afraid to approach them at first until the girls greeted them warmly. The couple was very confused because no one in the world talked to them. They had gotten used to being ignored.

Noticing the pouch they had, the married couple asked for some food. The girls freely gave all the food that was in the pouch to them. The couple was hesitant to take all the food, then the girls showed them that the pouch was full again after they poured out all the food. The couple had a confused look on their face, then the girls explained the endless bread supply that the Lord had given them. They explained that if the couple ate the bread, they would always be satisfied. They described the Lord's cottage and that the couple could have a warm home if they would come with them to the cottage. They would never have to leave and would always have a home. The couple was very suspicious at first because they questioned why the girls would even welcome them. They ate the bread and drank the wine, and immediately their hunger left them. As soon as they realized that they hungered no more, they rejoiced in the Truth that the girls were telling them and began to have faith in their words.

"'I am the living bread which came down from heaven. If anyone eats of this bread, he will live forever; and the bread that I shall give is My flesh, which I shall give for the life of the world.'"
    -    John 6:51 NKJV

"Oh, taste and see that the Lord is good; blessed is the man who trusts in Him!"
    -    Psalm 34:8 NKJV

Using the tiny book they had, they came back to the cottage. The Lord greeted them all and welcomed them with open arms. Realizing they would never have to want for anything again, the couple stayed and became like parents to the two girls. The couple joined in the teachings from the Lord, and they all grew in the Lord. The two girls got older and older and became beautiful women. Then it came time for them to go out again. The couple stayed at the cottage to help maintain a warm, loving home for when the girls came back. The Lord walked with them to the door, gave them the tiny book and bag of bread and wine, walked with them through the door, and sent them off again.

The girls walked through the forest searching for others they could tell about the cottage they grew up in, but couldn't find anyone who wanted to hear what they had to say. They walked for hours only to find no one who would listen. While they were looking for people, there was a rich man who took notice of them. He admired their beauty and greatly desired them. So he approached them to talk to them. They told him of their cottage that they inhabited, and he patiently listened. After he listened, he told them about his cottage that he also inhabited. They listened to him with interest and excitement because they thought that he too knew the Lord. So they followed him to his cottage.

They made it to his cottage and noticed that the cottage was seemingly bigger than the Lord's cottage but felt that something was off about it. He showed them around the cottage and all that he had. When they finished looking at the cottage, the rich man used this opportunity. "Please marry me. I saw both of you walking and was taken aback by your beauty. Leave that run down cottage that you live in and live with me. I can give you so much more than that supposed Lord can."

The two girls politely refused and tried to leave the cottage. Then the man continued to beg them as they were walking to the door. The girls rejected every one of his advances. Then at the last rejection, the man grew enraged. "Fine! If I can't have you, then there is no reason for anyone else to have you!" At those words, the rich man took the girls as prisoners and tried to force at least one of them to marry him locking them in a room. They remained steadfast in their answer, so this made the rich man very irate. He had never heard the word "no" before and had heard it seventy times seven from these lowly girls who had nothing. Not only that, but they chose someone who couldn't give them anything worthwhile. This enraged him, so he took the second girl...and killed her in his fury. After he killed her, he left the first girl in the room to think about her answer.

Heartbroken, the girl cried out. She remembered that the Lord had been with her and pleaded for a means of escape. Then through her watery eyes, the Lord showed her a secret passage in the walls that only the servants in the cottage knew about. She snuck through the tunnels and escaped from that cottage. Running through the forest, the girl didn't talk to anyone on her way. She didn't care about anyone at that point. She had just lost her sister and just wanted to go home to her refuge and never leave again.

She made it to the cottage. The Lord and the married couple greeted her at the door. They embraced her, and she cried in their arms over the loss of her dear sister. They walked into the cottage, and sitting at the kitchen table...she saw her dear sister that she had just lost! Relief washed over the girl's face as she saw that her sister was safe. They fell into each other's arms and cried over the pain that they had just experienced. Confused, the girl asked what happened.

Jesus: When you are in inhabitant in this cottage, no one completely dies and disappears. If you die in the world, you remain safe in this cottage forever. No matter what happens, you always come back here.

"For if we have been united together in the likeness of His death, certainly we also shall be in the likeness of His resurrection…"
- Romans 6:5 NKJV

In learning this, the girl understood that there was nothing to be afraid of because the Lord promised to take care of her. The days grew older and the girl grew more and more in the Lord. Her trust in Him grew stronger and stronger to where her boldness became endless.

"For to me, to live is Christ, and to die is gain."
- Philippians 1:21 NKJV

Then the time came for the girl to go out again into the world. She thought back on everything that had happened up until now. Thought about the cottage and how wonderful it was. She thought about the world and how cruel it could be. When these thoughts came, they all echoed the realization within her that the world and everyone in it needed the Lord's cottage. No one could live without it, and if someone died in the world without living in the cottage, then she didn't know what other cottage they would be trapped in. She walked to the door with the Lord. He gave her the tiny book to find her way back to the cottage and the pouch full of bread and wine. He walked with her through the door and out she went. With the resolve in her heart and the determination her eyes, she traveled through the forest again ready to share the message with the world about her Lord and His cottage. A resounding message that screamed...

"For God so loved the world that he gave His only begotten Son, that whoever believes in Him should not perish but have everlasting life."
-    John 3:16 NKJV

The Shining Bell Tower

"He who has an ear, let him hear what the Spirit says to the churches."
-    Revelation 2:29 NKJV

Here ye! Here ye! Come one! Come all! For the Glorious King is on His way! Blessed be the day He comes! Oh that blessed, glorious, wonderful day! Prepare for the coming King for He is near! Near ye! Near ye! The coming King is near!

We come to a simple, ordinary village. The name didn't stand out, there were no prominent landmarks, and the buildings were decades old. Just like every other village, this no-name town was steeped in darkness. There was almost no Light to be seen in any corner or crevice, and just like the town, the people were steeped in darkness. Each of the inhabitants were as twisted and wicked as the last.

Except one woman...
She was a simple, old, kind-hearted woman, who loved everyone in her village despite their twisted natures. Unlike everyone in her village, she wasn't surrounded in darkness. No. In fact, darkness fled when she was in the area. It fled because of the Light she carried. She was the only one that lived in Light and the only one that carried Light.

Every day, she would leave her house carrying a small oil lamp to try and encourage her people to walk in the Light.

"But if one walks in the night, he stumbles, because the light is not in him."
-    John 11:10 NKJV

Because she was the only one that carried the Light, the other villagers would become irritated when she walked past them. They have gotten so used to the darkness that it was shocking to see a sudden ray of Light. So much so that they came to hate the brightness.

"But the path of the just is like the shining sun, that shines ever brighter unto the perfect day. The way of the wicked is like darkness; they do not know what makes them stumble."
-    Proverbs 4:18-19 NKJV

"Come out of your houses, my people. There is nothing to fear," she would say. "There is no need to fear the Light. The Light is beautiful and wonderful."

But her kind words would always fall on deaf ears. Until one day, she decided to ring the bell. She walked up to the bell tower with her oil lamp and began to ring and shout words of joy and celebration:

Here ye! Here ye! Come one! Come all! For the Glorious King is on His way! Blessed be the day He comes! Prepare for the coming King for He is near! Near ye! Near ye! The coming King is near!

Every morning, noon, and night she would faithfully ring the bell and shout to share the Good News of the Light. The bell sounded beautiful to the old woman, but it was only noise to the villagers.

"For the message of the cross is foolishness to those who are perishing, but to us who are being saved it is the power of God."
    -    1 Corinthians 1:18 NKJV

One day, the villagers became angry and had enough of the old woman's clanging. "Knock out that racket, you old hag! We don't want to hear anything you have to say!"

"This is not clanging. It is the Heavenly bell of my coming King. I shall ring it until He comes."

"Well, your ringing, shouting, and shining is annoying the rest of us. Cut it out!"

"You have no eyes to see and ears to hear the beauty of my words. Woe to those who refuse to hear."

During the time that the woman wasn't ringing, the townspeople began to plot against her. As they were plotting, there was one townsman that began to heed the old woman's words and tried to defend her.

"She is doing no harm. Leave her alone. All she is doing is celebrating, and the Light she carries actually helps us to see the pathways in this town."

But those kind words fell on deaf ears as they continued to plot. A few days later, after they plotted, they decided to confront the old woman without the townsman that heeded her words. When the old woman began to make her walk to the bell tower, the wicked townspeople confronted her.

"Are you going to ring that annoying bell again?" Asked the townspeople.

"Certainly," said the old woman.

"Stop ringing that bell or else."

"No," said the old woman. "I will continue to ring until my Wonderful King comes."

So she walked to the bell tower with her oil lamp as the townspeople followed her. She picked up the mallet to prepare to ring the bell, but at that moment...the townspeople attacked her. Jostling her around, beating her, and throwing the oil lamp to the ground. The old woman knew what this meant...

"Father, forgive them, for they do not know what they do."
    -    Luke 23:34 NKJV

And so nothing was left of the old woman except the shattered oil lamp on the ground. The Light that was in the lamp was still burning brightly. The righteous townsman that heeded her words came to the bell tower after everything had transpired and saw the Light still burning in the shattered oil lamp. With tears of grief streaming down his cheeks, the righteous townsman picked up the shattered oil lamp and brought it home.

The next day...
That same righteous townsman walked out of his house with the same oil lamp the old woman carried. The lamp may have been shattered, but in his hands, it was like new as if it had never been touched. And so, in the presence of all the wicked townspeople, the righteous townsman walked the same narrow path to the bell tower that the old woman walked and said this as he rang the bell:

Here ye! Here ye! Come one! Come all! For the Glorious King is on His way! Blessed be the day He comes! Oh that blessed, glorious, wonderful day! Prepare for the coming King for He is near! Near ye! Near ye! The coming King is near!

Get Out While You Can

We've all heard the analogy of the burning building when it comes to telling others about the Gospel. We've all heard the comparison of you warning someone about eternal judgement being similar to you running around the building that is on fire knocking on everyone's door. It is a pretty good analogy, but not very realistic...let's expand on it.

Imagine that there is this huge apartment complex. It is seemingly the nicest building in the entire city. The complex has everything you could ever think of or want. You have people of all types living there: people living alone, people living with friends, people living with family, newlyweds, families with kids—a number of different households. Everything is peaceful as people carry on with their lives.

One day, in that same complex, someone decided to go to the top of the building and set a fire. This wasn't just a dumpster fire that someone forgot to put out. No. This particular person lit a small flame in the corner of the roof and walked away. Then that same person left the building and disappeared. The clock started. The events that followed that first spark were even more baffling than the person starting the fire.

As soon as the fire was lit, there were those people on different floors, who could immediately smell the kindle. Some of them may have looked the arson in the eye and

walked past him but didn't even know it. All they knew
was that they were sure that they smelled smoke
somewhere in the building. They started to investigate
the building keeping an eye out for any strange smells.
While these people investigated, they mentioned the
strange smell of smoke in the area. As they mentioned the
smoke, people laughed it off. "Smoke? *snicker* Buddy, I
think you're imagining things."

"...knowing this first: that scoffers will come in the last
days, walking according to their own lusts..."
   -   2 Peter 3:3 NKJV

Even though these people supposedly had the nose of a
bloodhound and are sure they smelled smoke, they begin
to doubt themselves. "Maybe you're right. I'm probably
just tired."

"'The sower sows the word. And these are the ones by the
wayside where the word is sown. When they hear, Satan
comes immediately and takes away the word that was
sown in their hearts.'"
   -   Mark 4:14-15 NKJV

After saying this, some of them listened to their loved
ones and stopped investigating. The kindle began to burn
more, so the smell of smoke started to get stronger. The
ones that continued to investigate began to feel
uncomfortable and slowly migrated to the exit. Some that
didn't listen the first time began to smell the smoke and
became more alert.

The kindle has now progressed to a small flame as the clock continued to tick to its untimely end. The now small flame began to really give off smoke. People not only smelled the smoke now, but they could even see the smoke. As some residents of the complex began to realize this, they began to panic. "Hey. I think there's a fire somewhere," said one of the residents. A few heeded that comment and began to rush toward the exit. Some residents stayed in their apartments ignoring the warnings. "I guess someone burned their dinner. They really need to open a window. It stinks in here," they said. The residents that heeded the words began to urgently knock on the doors of their neighbors telling them to exit the building. Some still ignored the warnings and others left everything behind to get out of the building.

Time ticked on as the fire grew to a roaring flame. The residents could smell the smoke, they could see the smoke, now came the heat. "Okay. There is definitely a fire. I am getting out of here!" Said some residents as they made a break for the door with their families. Some stubborn residents still remained in their apartments thinking that someone needed to turn on the A/C. So they continued carrying on as the fire steadily but quickly grew around them. A few brave residents that smelled the smoke and felt the heat attempted to search for the fire with fire extinguishers in hand, but realized that they were horribly unprepared. After realizing this, they quickly left the building to call for the Calvary while some residents, who had too much of an A/C dependency remained in their apartments oblivious to the horrible fate that they could face.

Time quickly progressed, and now visible flames that once were small have started to engulf the building burning everything in sight. As the building began to burn, the Calvary arrived. Those same residents, who were underprepared came back with the Fire Chief and gear to help them in the fire.

"Put on the whole armor of God, that you may be able to stand against the wiles of the devil."
-    Ephesians 6:11 NKJV

The Fire Chief began to give instructions to His new firemen...

"And He said to them, 'Go into all the world and preach the gospel to every creature. He who believes and is baptized will be saved; but he who does not believe will be condemned.'"
-    Mark 16:15-16 NKJV

With those Words, the firemen sprung into action charging towards the building wearing their fire gear.

The firemen entered the building and were grateful that they had their gear. The heat in the hallways was so hot that any person would get heat stroke from the outrageous temperature. The heat alone reminded them that their home was indeed burning.

"Stand therefore, having girded your waist with truth,
having put on the breastplate of righteousness,…"
-	Ephesians 6:14 NKJV

The floor was so hot that anyone with normal shoes
would have gotten third degree burns.

"…and having shod your feet with the preparation of the
gospel of peace…"
-	Ephesians 6:15 NKJV

The fire now covered every corner and started to burst
out of the walls.

"…above all, taking the shield of faith with which you will
be able to quench all the fiery darts of the wicked one."
-	Ephesians 6:16 NKJV

The firemen rushed through the hallways to search for
families that needed help. One of the firemen made it to
one of the apartments and heard coughing on the other
side. They tried to open the door, but it wouldn't budge.
So they took the ax they carried with them and began to
hack at the door. Grateful that they were able to breath
while chopping they quickly hacked the door to pieces.

"And take the helmet of salvation, and the sword of the
Spirit, which is the word of God;…"
-	Ephesians 6:17 NKJV

The fireman entered the apartment and found one of their neighbors coughing in the corner. The resident was so relieved to see them and immediately left with them. Another fireman found a family. They were quickly able to get the family out just in time before the ceiling collapsed in that apartment.

"'But these are the ones sown on good ground, those who hear the word, accept it, and bear fruit...''
   -   Mark 4:20 NKJV

Some residents, however, remained in their stubborn ways. Despite the fire burning around them, they refused to leave. Some even went so far as to say that there was never a fire in the building and that there never will be a fire. They kicked the firemen out of their apartments and locked the door behind them.

In the last apartment in the building, most of the family wanted to come but didn't want to leave their family who didn't believe that there was a fire. So they decided to stay with the family that didn't believe.

"'Now these are the ones sown among thorns; they are the ones who hear the word, and the cares of this world, the deceitfulness of riches, and the desires for other things entering in choke the word, and it becomes unfruitful.'"
   -   Mark 4:18-19 NKJV

The firemen got all the neighbors they could and quickly evacuated the building before they got stuck. Once they made it outside the building, the firemen tended to the saved residents dousing them with water to cool them down from the heat while the Fire Chief gave out His final warning. "The building is about the collapse. I strongly urge you to evacuate the premises immediately!" Instead of heeding the warnings of the Fire Chief, the remaining residents shouted insults at the Fire Chief. The residents that wanted to go went, and the ones that chose to stay remained. And I know you know what happened next...the entire building burned down.

This is what I believe would be an accurate analogy of the burning building. Now let me ask you something. Do you know why the firemen didn't drag those people who refused to believe that there was, in fact, a fire out of the building? That question can be answered with two responses. The first answer is that you can't force someone to believe that they are in danger. The only thing you can do is urge them to take heed in your words. If the firemen tried to spend time convincing those residents that their apartment was clearly about to burn to the ground, they would have wasted time they could have used to save others. The second answer is that if said firemen stayed and carried on with the stubborn residents in an attempt to convince them to leave, they would in turn have endangered themselves.

"Jesus said to him, 'Let the dead bury their own dead, but you go and preach the kingdom of God'"

-    Luke 9:60 NKJV

Another question I have for you...Have you considered why the firemen didn't just put out the fire? I can also answer that for you. The fire is sin consuming the world, and the building collapsing is God's Judgement. You can't slow down His imminent Judgement. You can't stop it. The only thing you can do is trust in the Way of escape, which is through Jesus Christ, the Fire Chief.

"Moreover, brethren, I declare to you the gospel which I preached to you, which also you received and in which you stand, by which also you are saved, if you hold fast that word which I preached to you—unless you believed in vain. For I delivered to you first of all that which I also received: that Christ died for our sins according to the Scriptures, and that He was buried, and that He rose again the third day according to the Scriptures,..."
-    1 Corinthians 15:1-4 NKJV

With that said, I urge anyone reading these words to heed the same words that the Fire Chief and the firemen represent in this story. Heed the words of the Gospel of Jesus Christ, and get out while you still can.

Heavenly Highway

The road to salvation is like a highway. You are in a car that someone lent you, and you are driving this highway alone. It's just you in the car. Others can follow behind you, but no one can ride in the car with you. The highway goes on and on for thousands of miles with no end in sight.

So on this highway, there is no speed limit. You can go as fast or as slow as your car will allow you to go. Some people will decide to drive this road as fast as they can to their own detriment. In the twists and turns of this highway, they run the risk of crashing on the side of the road or causing others to crash. Knowing this, you choose to not drive like a maniac and drive slower.

Just like the dangers of driving in real life, the dangers still apply in this faith highway. You have to stay focused on the road if you want to make it to your destination. If you fall asleep, you will crash the car. If you allow yourself to be distracted, you will crash the car. If you take detours that lead you to "supposed" shortcuts, you will eventually get lost. Sure it may be fun for a while, but after a certain point, being lost causes you to worry.

On this highway, everyone has the same GPS that works the exact same and tells everyone the exact same directions: Stay the straight and narrow. Do not turn to the right or to the left.

"Because narrow is the gate and difficult is the way which leads to life, and there are few who find it."
-    Matthew 7:14 NKJV

It doesn't matter if the road is bumpy or mountainous, stay on the straight and narrow. Unfortunately, there are those that don't like this road, which is understandable. It's not the most pleasant road to travel, but you travel the road with hopeful expectation in the destination.

As you are traveling this road, you follow the GPS that tells you to stay on the highway. Then suddenly, you start to feel completely exhausted. You grow weary. You begin to wonder if it would be okay to shut your eyes for just one moment to rest. Your head begins to nod, and the car begins to swerve. The tire shrieks, jerk you awake at the same time that a car is passing you. You look at the driver and notice that he too was feeling weary from the journey. The only difference was that he decided to close his eyes. You honk your horn and try to wake him, but it's too late. He's fast asleep and begins to swerve closer to your car. In a quick decision, you floor the gas to prevent collision with his car. The weary man veers off to the side and crashes into a tree. The car immediately catches on fire. You look in the rearview mirror in horror and continue on realizing that you shouldn't fall asleep.

To relieve your exhausted body and mind, you make it to a rest stop on the side of the highway and get out to stretch your legs. You walk around in the green grass, sit at a picnic table, and take in the sunlight before getting back on the road.

"The Lord is my shepherd; I shall not want. He makes me to lie down in green pastures; He leads me beside the still waters. He restores my soul; He leads me in the paths of righteousness for His name's sake."
-    Psalm 23:1-3 NKJV

You continue to venture down the road. After so many miles, you begin to see exit signs for many detours leading to "easier" ways to your destination. You consider taking some of them, but the exits that you pass always have traffic, so you continue on. Then you make it to an exit with no traffic. As soon as you turn onto the exit, the GPS calculates the change and leads you to many turns that will get you back on track. You ignore the directions and look around the road that you had just turned on. All of the places look interesting, but nothing really catches your eye. Until you get to one building that prompts you to stop.

You go in the building and explore a bit. You leave the building and try to get back on the road. As you drive, you realize that your GPS hasn't given you any directions for a while. You look at your GPS and realize that you have lost the signal. You have been wandering aimlessly on the detour road. You realize that you are horribly lost and continue to panic. You continue down the road trying to look for people that know the way back to the Heavenly Highway, but no one knows. In fact, all of the people you ask respond with, "There is no such road around here." Understanding that no one on the detour will be of any help, you continue travelling on the road hoping that the signal will come back for your GPS to work.

Then you realize that you had been travelling in only one direction, away from the Heavenly Highway. At this revelation, you look for places to turn around. As you are looking for places to turn, you begin to see many signs that say, "Heavenly Highway Loop 10 miles ahead." You feel relief as you continue on the road looking for the loop. Then you see a lost traveler parked on the side of the road. You stop and talk to him. You find out that he is also looking for the Heavenly Highway, but wasn't able to find the entrance. You tell him about the sign you just saw, and he is grateful for it and drives toward the loop. You travel further down and see another traveler on the side of the road. You tell him about the Heavenly Highway, but he immediately rejects your directions and drives the opposite way back to the detour site.

You continue down the road and eventually make it back to the Heavenly Highway. Getting on the highway, you notice that people are going faster than they probably should. You see a group of cars driving three times the speed limit and begin to swerve into each other. Then at some point, they collide with each other and swerve off the highway. Their cars catch on fire, but they miraculously survive. After their crash, you see them start to walk on the side of the road in your rearview mirror. You continue on and eventually make it to the end of the Heavenly Highway, and it is much more wonderful than you could ever have imagined. It is definitely worth the crazy trip.

"Eye has not seen, nor ear heard, nor have entered into the heart of man the things which God has prepared for those who love Him."
- 1 Corinthians 2:9 NKJV

The Path

Imagine a world where there are many roads. There are all types of crazy roads. Some roads take you down through the valleys, the forests, and the mountains. Some roads take you way up in the clouds. Some roads are as topsy-turvy as life. Taking you every which way with many loops and corkscrews. The people of this world all travel on these roads at the speed that they choose with different means of transportation. Some use bikes. Some use skateboards. Some use cars. Some take community buses. Very few take the humblest of all modes of transportation...walking. If you walked, you were considered as very strange.

Where these roads went nobody knew. Each person traveling on these roads felt that they were going the right way. So they traveled as they saw fit. Until one day, a young woman was traveling at break neck speed in her car and got into an accident. It was a really bad accident that totaled her car and threw her onto the road. "What happened?!" She said to herself. She looked around to see what had caused the accident and noticed that her car ran over a turtle shell. The turtle was perfectly fine, but she couldn't say much about her car. There she sat on the side of the road with her injuries from the accident hoping for someone to help, however, anyone who saw her sped past her.

As a result of her injuries, she was too weak to continue her travels on the road she was on. So she decided to look for another way. She slowly walked on the side of the road with cars whizzing by her until she came to a single, narrow, dirt path in the midst of all the roads and highways.

Curious as to where the path came from, she walked up to the entrance. Before she stepped on the path, a Gatekeeper walked into view.

Gatekeeper: Where are you going?

Woman: I am unable to travel on any other roads. I don't have any means of transportation, and it is too dangerous for me.

Gatekeeper: Before you go any further, I must warn you that on this road, you only walk. There is no other means to traverse this path. If you choose this road, you must know that it is the hardest road to travel. It is not for the faint of heart. Are you sure you want to start your journey on this path?

Curious as to what awaited her, the woman answered, "Yes. I am sure.".

Gatekeeper: Okay. Just know that this path will not be easy for you to travel, but if you choose to travel this path and endure to the end, the destination will be much greater than you could ever imagine.

"Because narrow is the gate and difficult is the way which leads to life, and there are few who find it."
-    Matthew 7:14 NKJV

"But he who endures to the end shall be saved."
-    Matthew 24:13 NKJV

"I must also give you this," said the Gatekeeper as he hands the woman a map. "This map will show you all the places that you should never go on this path." The woman looked at the map and noticed that every road was marked in red. "Sir, every road outside of this road is marked in red. Are you saying that these roads and the road I was just on are roads that one should never traverse?" The Gatekeeper gave her a dark look and warned her, "It is by the Grace of God that you were taken off that road, for it would have led to your destruction."

"Enter by the narrow gate; for wide is the gate and broad is the way that leads to destruction, and there are many who go in by it."
-    Matthew 7:13 NKJV

The woman trembled at those words and heeded the warning.

Gatekeeper: I must also give you a Compass. Do you believe the map and everything that I have told you thus far?

Woman: Yes.

Gatekeeper: Do you trust that what this map says is true? Do you trust it with your life?

Woman: Yes.

Gatekeeper: Okay. You may proceed.

"...that if you confess with your mouth the Lord Jesus and believe in your heart that God has raised Him from the dead, you will be saved. For with the heart one believes unto righteousness, and with the mouth confession is made unto salvation."
   -    Romans 10:9-10 NKJV

At these words, the woman felt a peace wash over her that she couldn't comprehend.

Woman: Wait. Where is the Compass? You said there was a Compass.

"You already have it," said the Gatekeeper. The woman looked at the Gatekeeper with a very confused look. "You will understand as you travel on the path," said the Gatekeeper.

"In Him you also trusted, after you heard the word of truth, the gospel of your salvation; in whom also, having believed, you were sealed with the Holy Spirit of promise,..."

- Ephesians 1:13 NKJV

The woman, still confused, took her first steps on the path with a new found strength. She continued to walk along the path following the map until she got to her first fork in the road. The fork presented two paths that had drastically different appearances. The path on the right led back to the highway system that she once traveled, and the path on the left led down a dark, downward slope. Looking at the map, she was confused. She could see that the path on the right was marked in red, but she was sure that the path on the left was the wrong way to go. As she was about to take a step to the right leading back to the old road, someone suddenly whispered.

Voice: Take the path on the left.

"Who said that?" Confused, the woman looked around, but no one was in sight. "That's strange. I am sure I heard a voice." Walking towards the path on the right, she heard the whisper again.

Voice: Don't take that path. You will perish if you take that path.

Turning to the voice, someone came into view. There stood before her a Man. This wasn't your average Man. He was someone who seemed to have a Light inside of Him. Even though He stood next to the darkness, it was as if the road was lit by the sun. As she stared at Him, the woman felt absolute peace. It was as if she had known Him all her life even though she had just met Him.

Woman: Why do you say that? Don't you see that road? It is completely dark. The right is obviously the way.

Man: Why do you say that? It clearly leads back to where you came. It is a dead end. What does your map say?

Woman: It says to go down the path on the left.

Man: Then we should go down the path on the left.

Woman: But even if that is the way, it's too dark for me to pass through. I can just take the path on the right and circle back to another part of this road.

Man: That path is a dead end. It won't do you any good. You'll get too confused to even make it back to this path.

Woman: Then what do you suppose I do?

Man: Trust my Words. Trust the map that I drew out.

Woman: You drew this map?

Man: Yes. I will even walk with you. I know you're scared, but I will be with you all the way to the end.

"Trust in the Lord with all your heart, and lean not on your own understanding; in all your ways acknowledge Him, and He shall direct your paths."
-    Proverbs 3:5-6 NKJV

The woman looked at this Man and the hand extended to her. A nudge within her was pointing straight to Him and was urging her to trust Him. Leaning into this push within her, she took His hand, and they began to walk down the dark path together.

As they walked down the slope, the path lit up. It was as if she could see everything on the path. All of the obstacles and traps that had been laid out for unsuspecting travelers. All of them untouched. As they walked, the woman talked to the Man and got to know Him. She learned that His name was Jesus Christ and that He was the shepherd for this road. He walked with everyone who traveled this path and all of them who decided to stay with Him made it to the end.

They had been peacefully walking along until they came to a point in the path where it touched the other roads. The path she had been on was the rockiest it had ever been.

Woman: Jesus, this path has so many rocks in it. Maybe we should use the other road to bypass this one. My feet hurt.

Jesus: No. We will stay on this road. Don't even dip a single toe on that road.

Woman: I don't see the problem. Look this road travels the same way as this path. Let's walk on the smoother path for now and then get back on this road when it smooths out.

The woman tried to move them toward the other path, but Jesus held her hand even tighter and prevented her from moving forward.

Jesus: What did the Gatekeeper ask you at the start of your travels?

Woman: If I trusted the map?

Jesus: What does the map say?

Woman: That the path next to us is the wrong way, but you wrote the map.

Jesus: Does that make the map any less true?

Woman: No.

With those words, the woman continued on the rocky path.

As they continued to walk, the woman talked to Jesus about the other paths. She questioned why He told her to never set foot on those paths. He explained that all of the other roads lead to the same place. Destruction. Complete separation and torment. The reason you couldn't see the end was because if people really saw where they were going, then they would all flock to the narrow, dirt road. It was all designed by the person who created the road system around the dirt path. The enemy who doesn't want anyone to know that all roads outside of the dirt path only lead to destruction. Total, absolute darkness. In the name of progress and advancement, the roads got more and more complicated. As soon as they started saying that the dirt road was too old, they built new roads. More and more roads were added until they became the highway system. "But if that is the case, why can't we see the end of the dirt road?" Asked the woman.

Jesus: You can't see the end of the dirt road because if you saw the end, you would then see all that you would have to pass. In turn, that would cause you to look for another road to travel. That would then lead you to another destination then where you wanted to go.

They continued to travel, then they came to a point where it seemed like the roads were traveling the same way again. There was a small chasm between them. The other road came into view as a crowd of people passed by. They saw the woman and asked, "Do you need a ride? You seem tired." "A ride would be very nice. Thank you," said the woman. The woman tried to step forward, but Jesus held her back again. "They are offering a ride. They are nice people. They'll drop us off further ahead," said the woman. "Those people will be too concerned with driving on that fast-paced road to notice anything. You found this path once. It will be hard to find it again if you leave it." The woman looked at the other path again, but this time she began to see. The two paths were not side by side anymore. There was now a small chasm wide enough to where she would have to jump to make it to each road.

Jesus: That chasm will be almost impossible to cross.

At these words, the woman continued on the dirt path only to come to a treacherous mountain. "Oh no," said the woman. "I am not climbing that. Don't you see how dangerous that is. That mountain is a rockslide waiting to happen. Then where would we be?" "Just trust Me. You will be fine," said Jesus. Jesus then proceeds to lead her up the mountain step by step. He always made sure to take the first step then instructing her to follow His exact steps. "Keep your head down," He warned. "If you put your head up too high, you will be hit in the head by falling rocks." They slowly and carefully traveled up the mountain. There were a few rockslides. However, when they occurred, the boulders were either crushed as they hit Jesus, or they found caves within the incline to hide in as the rockslide passed.

After all of the hardships that Jesus and the woman had overcome, a fear in the woman began to grow at the expectation of what was left in the travels. So much so that she longed to be on the old road. "I would love to go back to that path. It was so much easier," she thought.

When she saw the old path in her eyes once again, she desperately wanted to get back to that path.

Jesus: I know what you are thinking. Don't go back to that path. If you go back now, it will be even more dangerous than before.

Woman: But that path was so much easier. Why don't we just walk on that path for just a little while?

Jesus: That path is more dangerous now than it was before. You don't belong on that path. Stay on this one where it's safer.

Woman: Safer?! What do you mean safer?! Even since I've been on this path, I've felt nothing but discomfort and fear. My feet are sore from walking. I have blisters on the bottom of my feet! Not only that, I've been clonked in the head by falling rocks too many times! I have bumps on my head because we climbed that mountain! I want to go back to the easier path!

As the woman said this, she let go of Jesus's hand that she had been holding this whole time and began to sprint toward the edge of the path. As she made it to the edge of the path, she jumped across the chasm and just barely made it to the other side.

As soon as she got to the other side, she looked back at Jesus, who stayed in that same spot on the other path. The strong nudge was still pointing at Him as she stared into His warm eyes that were pleading for her to jump back to the other side. She broke eye contact and ran away crying. As she was running away, that strong nudge still urged her to turn around, but she ignored it.

Without a car and no companion to talk to, she continued walking on the other road and realized that she wasn't going to get anywhere without transportation. So she began to hitchhike. The woman tried to hitchhike and managed to flag down a couple cars, but every car that stopped for her, she refused to get in. The strong nudge stopped her every time, so it didn't feel right for her to get in the car. Realizing that hitchhiking wouldn't work, she resolved to just continue walking. With every step she took, the strong nudge got weaker and weaker. She could barely feel the nudge until she came to a bus stop and got on the bus. The nudge pointing her in the opposite direction was still weak as she got on the bus and got weaker and weaker.

As she rode the bus, she felt that something was off. She looked out the window and noticed that the view outside was getting darker and darker until it was so thick that you could feel the darkness around you. As she noticed the darkness getting thicker and thicker, she noticed that the bus was driving faster and faster at the same time. She began to panic and tried to find a way off the bus. She proceeded to break the window and jumped out the bus. It was a miracle that she survived the jump after landing on the side of the road. Cold, alone, and more afraid than she had ever been, the woman began to mourn for the loss of the company that she once had in Jesus. She sat there crying on the road wishing that she could see Him again and be at His side again. At those thoughts, the woman suddenly felt the nudge get stronger. It began to push her back the way she came. Gathering her strength, she proceeded to painfully limp back the way she came. The occasional car passed by her in the darkness, and a couple drivers offered her rides the other way, but she ignored them all and followed the nudge that began to grow stronger and stronger again.

The pain from the fall grew with every step, but she didn't care. All she could think about was being at Jesus's side again. She came back to the same spot that she left Jesus and saw Him still standing exactly where she had left Him waiting for her to return. When she saw Him, she dropped to her knees and began to weep. She was so happy that He was still there for her despite the fact that she left Him. Because of her weakness, she couldn't jump to the other side, so Jesus jumped over, picked her up, and jumped back to the other side.

Jesus put her down on the dirt road. In her broken state, she looked at Jesus. She noticed that He had been walking for so long that He walked on blisters that burst and bled on His feet. She looked at His hands and noticed that there were holes in His hands from the shards of boulders that fell on Him when He protected her. She saw this and began to weep very loudly. She thanked Jesus for protecting her and walking with her, and she apologized for how she had acted. He forgave her, and once she regained her strength, they continued on.

"If we confess our sins, He is faithful and just to forgive us our sins and to cleanse us from all unrighteousness."
-    1 John 1:9 NKJV

They had a long conversation about what just transpired. Jesus knew where she had gone and how far she had gone. He explained to her that the darkness she was in was the darkness of the world leading to destruction. He told her that if the Gatekeeper had not given her the Compass, she would have been completely lost in the world's darkness never to have found the path again. He also told her that if she had gone far enough, she would have never heard the Compass again and would have remained lost.

The woman was then very grateful and held Jesus's hand very tightly. As Jesus and the woman continued on the trail, they faced many more trials together. The only difference is that the woman never once complained about the trials again because she learned that the trials were better than the darkness that she had witnessed and was thankful that Jesus was there with her. This continued on until they made it to the end. The destination was indeed far greater than she could have ever imagined. As she finished her journey, she hoped that someone else on those twisted roads would find the dirt path and begin their travels on it. She knew that she would have never made it without Jesus, and that was something that she would forever be grateful for.

"Jesus said to him, 'I am the way, the truth, and the life. No one comes to the Father except through Me.'"
-    John 14:6 NKJV

The Deceptive Castle

In a gorgeous countryside with rolling hills and tall grass, we come to a beautiful maiden, who was betrothed to her Groom. She always walked with Him, and wherever He went, there she was also. He loved her, and you could say she dearly loved Him. He always kept His word, and she always remained faithful to Him.

One day, they were walking hand in hand on a narrow path through a beautiful forest full of trees. As they were walking, they suddenly came to mansion. It was a beautiful house with many rooms full of life. A beautiful, lush garden on the side full of many hedges and rose bushes. There was a winding, broad path large enough for a car that led to a gigantic driveway right up to the front door.

"Enter by the narrow gate; for wide is the gate and broad is the way that leads to destruction, and there are many who go in by it. Because narrow is the gate and difficult is the way which leads to life, and there are few who find it."
-    Matthew 7:13-14 NKJV

This mansion caught the eyes of the maiden, and she stopped, still holding her Groom's hand.

"What is it, my love?" Said the Groom.

"That castle. It's beautiful. I would love to live in a place like that."

As she said this, she could hear lively music and see people scurrying past the many windows of the house and frolicking in the front lawn. The maiden stared in wonder and enchantment at the supposed happiness and excitement. The Groom looked at the scene in front of them and was not amused.

"Pay no attention to that, my love. For that is only a trap for the lion's den. I have a house with many rooms, and I offer far more for you than what you see right now. Just stay with Me."

"In My Father's house are many mansions; if it were not so, I would have told you. I go to prepare a place for you."
   -   John 14:2 NKJV

The maiden stares at the path hesitantly, wishing to explore the house, but nonetheless, she kept walking with her Groom hand in hand. Then at nightfall, as the maiden was trying to sleep, she tossed and turned. She could still hear the lively music. She began to wonder, "How can we hear music even though we've travelled such a great distance?" That's it! She had it. Her curiosity got the better of her. She looked at the Groom peacefully sleeping next to her, and managed to sneak away. "My Groom will never know of my absence. I'll be back before the day's first light," she thought.

The maiden ran on the path to the castle. As she came closer and closer to the castle, the path she was on grew wider and wider. "I must be going the right way," she said. And then…she saw the light from the castle in the distance.

As she walked down the path to the front door, she heard the music and the sound of laughter growing louder and louder. She made it to the front door that was made of beautiful mahogany wood, and knocked. She waited. Then suddenly…a man opened the door. This man was dressed in a full black suit that looked like it was from the most expensive store. The maiden took a good look at him and was surprised to see that he looked so much like her Groom, but there was something off about him. Something that made him completely different from her Groom despite the fact that he looked like Him.

"Welcome, my sweet," he said with a mischievous voice. "What brings you here?"

"I heard music and was just curious about what was going on."

"Well, you seem a long way from home. Wouldn't your Groom be upset that you left Him?", the mysterious man said.

"I don't have a Groom."

"Well, that is swell, my sweet. Come on in and join the party. Look around and enjoy yourself. You may find that you won't be able to leave once you see all there is to see…"

So the maiden hesitantly stepped over the threshold of the door and entered the castle. It was like she stepped into a new world of people that lived completely different lives from her life. She looked around as she walked with the mysterious man. She saw people of all shapes and sizes gathered in different parts of the house with the most extravagant outfits that no normal person would wear. The maiden didn't have a good feeling about the world she had just stepped into, but nonetheless she kept walking.

The maiden walked with the man through many parts of the castle until he led her to a room.

"A lady must always be dressed for the occasion. There are beautiful clothes for you that fit the occasion of the party."

With that, he kissed her hand at her slight discomfort and left her. His servants whisked her into the room and prepped her for the party. As the servants helped her to get dressed, they showered her with empty compliments on her amazing beauty.

"My! You are such a catch, lovely. Are you sure there is no Groom?"

The maiden just smiled awkwardly at this question as they continued to dress her. They had finally finished dressing her and showed her reflection. There she stood in a beautiful, extravagant, pink dress. Perfect for the occasion of the party. The maiden marveled at her appearance in the mirror, but she couldn't bury the feeling of something not feeling right. Nonetheless, she carried on.

At this moment, the mysterious man walked in.

"My! You look absolutely gorgeous, my sweet."

The maiden couldn't help but awkwardly smile, thinking about her Groom she had left in the night.

"But, my sweet, there is still something missing...turn around."

She turned around, and the mysterious man surprised her with a large diamond necklace that glowed as bright as the moon. She looked at him in surprise, and he also gave her matching bracelets to put on her wrists. So the mysterious man put one bracelet on each wrist.

"The outfit is now complete. Now everyone will know that I am your one and only groom."

The maiden could tell the jewelry was very valuable since she could feel the weight on her arms and neck. So with her new look, she was escorted to the party by the mysterious man.

The maiden carried on at the party having light conversations with the guests, drinking the drinks that were offered, and eating the food that was given. With every sip taken, with every bite eaten, and with every word spoken, the maiden felt more and more uneasy.

"I have to get back to my Groom. I want to see my Love. I think the sun is almost up," she thought.

And with those thoughts, she made her way to the door.

She tried to open the door, but it wouldn't budge. She even tried jostling it, but it wouldn't open. At this point, the party had been brought to a halt, and everyone stopped to stare at her. The maiden started to feel a sense of fear wash over her as the mysterious man walked up to her.

"Where are you going, my sweet?"

"I must leave now. I must return to my Groom," she said.

"Oh no. I'm afraid you can't do that. Once you step through that threshold, you are mine. I am your one and only groom now."

With those words, the maiden began to see the truth. Everything started to shift. The glitz and glamor of the mansion began to shift into deteriorated junk. The people began to change form as if they weren't even human. Even the mysterious man himself, or should we say monster, began to change. His face started to shift and was contorted into the most horrific grin.

"You are mine now, my sweet. You aren't going anywhere."

And with that, the monster commanded his servants to take the maiden away. The servants grabbed some chains and pulled, and the maiden was jerked forward. She looked down and noticed that the necklace and bracelets changed into thick, heavy chains, and her dress turned into mere rags. So she was pulled along to be prepared to serve the monster for the rest of her life.

As she sat imprisoned in a room, the maiden was at a loss of what to do and felt so much despair and sorrow from what she had gotten herself into that she began to openly weep and pray.

"Where are you, my Groom? My Love. I am so sorry for leaving You. Please help me, Jesus."
"I've left Him, and now He will never take me back. If only I had listened to Him," she thought.

"For 'whoever calls on the name of the Lord shall be saved.'"
-   Romans 10:13 NKJV

At that moment, a Light began to glow near the maiden. She looked up and there was an intangible Light that shined brighter than the sun.

"Get up, My Love. We must go," the Light said.

"But how? Everything is locked. The windows, the door, and I can't break the windows or they will hear."

"Do you trust Jesus your Lord?"

"Trust in the Lord with all your heart, and lean not on your own understanding; in all your ways acknowledge Him, and He shall direct your paths."
-	Proverbs 3:5-6 NKJV

"I do," said the maiden.

At those words, there was then a sudden sound of the door unlocking and opening. The maiden stepped out of the room into the decrepit hallway and looked around. The castle was so twisted by this time that it was unrecognizable and very dim and dark compared to how it previously had been. The maiden looked beside the door and noticed that the guards were sound asleep. Instead of fear, she received a new found strength and began to run down the hall to find her freedom.

At that same moment, the monster was walking to her room from the other direction to make her serve him. Because the hallway was dark, he didn't see her running down the hall. He noticed the guards sleeping and the door open.

"FIND HER!" He yelled.

"SEARCH EVERY CORNER OF THIS MANSION UNTIL YOU FIND HER! BRING HER TO ME ALIVE."

The maiden heard this as she was running down the hall, and it only made her run faster. Then she suddenly began to hear growls around her as if there was a lion looking to devour her. She tried to find the path to the exit, but it was as if the house suddenly turned into a maze. At every corner she heard growls, so she had to constantly hide.

Then the Light shone next to her again.

"Trust Me and focus on Me," the Light said. So the maiden listened to the Light and ran down the hallway, not hearing any growls or finding any guards or servants. The Light led her right to the room where the exit was, and on the other side of the front door's threshold, she saw her Groom on a white horse.

She began to sprint faster, tears streaming down her eyes as she looked at her Groom from a distance. However, as she was running, she didn't just hear growls behind her, but a mighty lion's roar. She could sense that the lion was right on her heels as she ran faster than she had ever run in her entire life. Suddenly the Light that had been guiding her shined so brightly that it blinded the lion who shrieked in pain, and the maiden made it to the threshold and jumped through the door. As she crossed the threshold, the chains that were on her neck and wrists unlocked and fell to the ground, and her dress changed into a real white gown.

Jesus caught her in His arms and they got on the horse and left that prison of a castle. The maiden looked back and saw the castle change into what it really was...a broken down, old, condemned house. The lush garden on the side of the house turned into a garden of dead trees. The amazing exterior changed into an old paint job with missing roof shingles. The path that led to the door changed into a dirt road, and the beautiful mahogany door turned into a broken down, cheap wooden door hanging off its hinges. As they rode away, the maiden looked at the house to hear nothing. No people. No music. No castle. Just the view of a house full of death and desolation.

"For I, the Lord your God, am a jealous God..."
-    Exodus 20:5 NKJV

"You are Mine, My love. And that will never change," said the Groom.

Suddenly, the maiden began to shine with an inner Light that was brighter than the sun. The maiden looked at her Groom and realized that she had found her freedom. That freedom was in Him, and she was never letting that go again.

"I know that now, my Lord."

No Happy Ending

I'm going to let you in on a little secret.
There is no happy ending in this life.

Now I know that is a lot to take in, but it's true.
Let me explain.

In a world where we have so many ups and downs and hills and valleys, life is a roller coaster.
You're up one minute, but down the next.
That is what life is all about.
Life is about the good and the bad.

Still confused?
Okay. Let me explain it another way.
Imagine life is like a giant book.
Your life in particular.
Some people have books with many chapters, and some with few.
Some chapters are incredibly short.
Some chapters, however, feel like they drag on forever...
We all start from birth in the first chapter then move on through the book of our life.
Each stage of our life is a new chapter.
No chapter is the same for two people.
And what happens at the end of a chapter?
Well...it depends on the person.

Some chapters have amazing endings, while others have terrible endings.

As we close different chapters in our lives, we move on with the hope that the next chapter will be better than the last no matter how good or bad the previous chapter was.
We build up the book of our lives chapter by chapter.
Page after page until...
We reach the last page of the last chapter of the book of our life.
No matter who's book you are reading, be it your's or someone else's, they all end the same.
"They closed their eyes and took their last breath"...the end.
This is why I say there is no happy ending in this life because of that one inevitable, tragic ending that will crush anyone.
This life is filled with chapters where the best ending you can possibly get is a happy ending at the end of each chapter.
So there is no happy ending in this life.

But let me tell you a mystery...
It doesn't mean that you can never get a happy ending...
This life may not have a happy ending, but another life does.
Eternal life.
This is the life after death.
And that life can be found in Jesus Christ and only Jesus Christ.
He saves us with the sacrifice of the cross to give us His happy ending.

The only thing we have to do is believe in the free gift of His happy ending.

A happy ending full of eternal promises....

Eternal Peace...

Eternal fellowship...

Eternal love...

A happy ending where love and sacrifice literally conquers all.

So there is no happy ending in this life...

Because there is the Ultimate Happy Ending after life.

All you have to do...

Is just have faith in Jesus Christ and what He did on the cross, repent, turn to Him, and turn from your life of sin.

"But what does it say? 'The word is near you, in your mouth and in your heart' (that is, the word of faith which we preach): that if you confess with your mouth the Lord Jesus and believe in your heart that God has raised Him from the dead, you will be saved. For with the heart one believes unto righteousness, and with the mouth confession is made unto salvation. For the Scripture says, 'Whoever believes on Him will not be put to shame.' For there is no distinction between Jew and Greek, for the same Lord over all is rich to all who call upon Him. For 'whoever calls on the name of the Lord shall be saved.'"

- Romans 10:8-13 NKJV

THE ROAD TO SALVATION

1.) Admit that you are a sinner in need of a Savior.

2.) Believe in the Gospel of Jesus Christ.
   - He came as God in the flesh, was crucified for your sins, and rose from the dead.

     "For I delivered to you first of all that which I also received: that Christ died for our sins according to the Scriptures, and that He was buried, and that He rose again the third day according to the Scriptures,..."
   - 1 Corinthians 15:3-4 NKJV

3.) Publicly profess your new found faith

"...that if you confess with your mouth the Lord Jesus and believe in your heart that God has raised Him from the dead, you will be saved. For with the heart one believes unto righteousness, and with the mouth confession is made unto salvation."
   - Romans 10:9-10 NKJV

Thank you for reading this book of parables. I hope this book has encouraged you to be like these interesting characters and step out on faith. It doesn't matter how big or small your job is for the Kingdom of Heaven. God can use anything to carry the Gospel. I encourage you to seek out God and let Him show you the small task He wants you to do. So now that you have reached the end of this book...go. Do something for the Kingdom. Go on now. Go out into the forest proclaiming the love of God to all those who would listen. Go ring the bell at the bell tower warning others of the only Way to escape God's Judgement. You have already found the narrow, dirt road, now walk with Jesus on it, and help others to find it. I'll see you when the journey is over. :D

"...being confident of this very thing, that He who has begun a good work in you will complete it until the day of Jesus Christ;..."
-   Philippians 1:6 NKJV

www.ingramcontent.com/pod-product-compliance
Lightning Source LLC
Chambersburg PA
CBHW031212160726
47992CB00006B/2694